The Adventures of Goliath

Goliath Goes to Summer School

The Adventures of Goliath

Goliath Goes to Summer School

Terrance Dicks
Illustrated by
Valerie Littlewood

New York

First edition for the United States and the Philippines
published 1989 by Barron's Educational Series, Inc.

First published 1987 by Piccadilly Press Ltd., London, England

All inquiries should be addressed to:
Barron's Educational Series, Inc.
250 Wireless Boulevard
Hauppauge, New York 11788

Library of Congress Catalog Card No. 88-7765
International Standard Book No. 0-8120-4210-7

Library of Congress Cataloging-in-Publication Data
Dicks, Terrance.
Goliath goes to summer school/Terrance Dicks; illustrated by
Valerie Littlewood.
p. cm. — (The adventures of Goliath)
Summary: David's big dog, Goliath, follows him to summer
school on a farm and helps him to solve a ghostly mystery.
ISBN 0-8120-4210-7
[1. Mystery and detective stories. 2. Dogs—Fiction. 3. Schools—
Fiction.] I. Littlewood, Valerie, ill. II. Title. III. Series: Dicks,
Terrance. Adventures of Goliath.
PZ7. D5627Gtuv 1989
[E]—dc19   88-7765
                                                              CIP
                                                              AC

PRINTED IN THE UNITED STATES OF AMERICA

012 9770 987654321

CONTENTS

Chapter One

— and Goliath Came, Too!

"Now are you sure you've got everything?" asked David's mother for about the twentieth time.

David studied the printed list provided by the school. "Sneakers, gym shorts, socks, pants, shirts, rubber boots . . ." The list seemed endless. David rattled it all off, checking as he went along. "Yes. Don't worry, Mom. It's all there."

"And everything's labeled?"

David sighed. "Yes, it's all labeled." David's school was crazy about having things labeled—as if anyone was likely to want to steal his smelly old socks anyway, thought David.

The reason for all this fuss was that David was about to leave on an important school trip.

Not just a day trip but a whole week.

The school rented a place called Foskett's Farm every summer, and the different classes took turns spending a week there.

It was known as summer school, and although there were still some classes to go to, it was a lot more fun than ordinary school. Or so David had heard. This was to be his first trip, and he was really looking forward to it.

The only thing was, he felt sure he was going to miss Goliath. Goliath was David's dog, a massive, shaggy animal, part St. Bernard, part Irish wolfhound, part mastiff—part elephant, too, David's dad always said.

Goliath had grown from a tiny shivering puppy to one of the biggest and shaggiest dogs in the world, and he and David were devoted to each other.

Goliath, meanwhile, was sitting by the end of David's bed, studying the preparations, his head cocked to one side in puzzlement. Goliath couldn't quite figure out what was going on.

At first he'd though it must be vacation time.

Goliath loved vacations.

The family always took him along with them, and he loved seeing new places and meeting new people.

But if it was vacation time there would be lots more fuss with the whole family rushing around packing, and the car being loaded with luggage.

This time it was just David's old backpack that was being loaded—just David who seemed to be getting

ready for a trip.

Goliath wasn't the cleverest dog in the world.

In fact, to be honest, he was just a tiny bit dim-witted.

But he was very determined.

There was just one idea firmly fixed inside Goliath's big shaggy head.

If David was going somewhere, Goliath was going, too!

David's mother looked at her watch. "Time to go. Sure you can manage?"

David shrugged himself into the backpack. "Yes, it's not too heavy. Besides, it'll be good practice for me. Everyone says they make you walk miles and miles."

David gave his mother a kiss—his

dad had already set off for work.

Then he knelt down and gave Goliath a final hug and kiss as well. "Goodbye, Goliath. Don't worry, it'll soon go by."

Goliath gave him a puzzled look and licked his ear.

Wiping his face to dry it—Goliath's tongue felt like a wet washcloth—David hurried out of the house and headed for school, where the schoolbus was waiting.

Goliath tried to follow him, but David's mom grabbed him by the collar and heaved him back. It wasn't easy, because Goliath was far stronger than she was. "No, Goliath," she panted. "You're not going, not this time. Go and lie down and I'll take you for a nice walk later on."

Then they went downstairs into the kitchen.

David's mother started clearing up, and Goliath stretched out under the kitchen table, his head in his paws, trying to figure things out. David's father wasn't going away—he'd left for work earlier that morning as usual.

David's mom was still here, too, puttering about.

But David was gone.

And he hadn't just gone to school, either. There'd been too much good-bye business for that. And besides, he was carrying one of those mysterious bundles called luggage that humans insist on dragging with them when they go away anywhere.

Suddenly, Goliath realized the awful truth.

David was going away by himself—and he'd forgotten to take Goliath with him!

That wouldn't do at all, thought Goliath.

How was David going to manage without Goliath to look after him?

Some terrible mistake had been made, decided Goliath. It was up to him to put it right at once.

Goliath got up—then he sat down again.

David's mother didn't understand about the mistake.

She'd just try to stop him again.

Goliath got up again, slowly this time.

Step by step he crept cautiously out of the kitchen and through the open door into the backyard.

Once he was safely in the yard the rest was simple. He hurtled over the back fence into the next door garden. Ignoring the angry shouts of Mr. MacGregor, their next door neighbor,

who was working in his garden as usual, Goliath leaped over his garden gate which opened directly onto the street, and then he disappeared down the road . . .

*   *   *

David panted into the school playground where the schoolbus was waiting.

The backpack had seemed to get heavier and heavier, and thanks to that and to all the goodbyes, David was a bit late.

Second to last of the Mohicans

The rest of his class were already on the bus. They all set up a cheer as David arrived.

Miss Hollings, David's history teacher, was standing impatiently by the door. She was one of his favorite teachers—tall and thin and vague, and a tireless worker for good causes.

But this morning she was a bit frazzled. Being responsible for the outing was clearly getting on her nerves. "There you are, David! Do hurry up, we're late already."

David staggered onto the bus. "Sorry, Miss Hollings!"

Wriggling out of the backpack, he sat down next to his friend Tom, a bold-looking boy with red hair and freckles.

"Right, off you go then, driver," said Miss Hollings.

Quickly, the bus drove out of the

playground, turned into the traffic, and drove away.

Minutes later, Goliath thundered into the playground and looked around expectantly.

But there was no one there.

David had gone and Goliath was left all alone.

Chapter Two

On the Road

Goliath gave a mighty woof that rattled the windows of the school. Maybe David was inside. Maybe he'd hear him and come out.

Old Mr. Roberts, the caretaker, heard the racket and popped out of his little office just by the front door.

He knew Goliath well.

"Hello, old chap, what are you doing here?" Mr. Roberts laughed wheezily. "I'm afraid you're too late.

They've all gone! You've missed the bus!"

He led Goliath to the school gates and pointed to a yellow dot in the distance. "See, there they go! If you wanted to say goodbye to David, you're too late. You'd better go home."

Patting Goliath on the head, Mr. Roberts went back into his office. Goliath sat down on the sidewalk, hanging his head.

Then suddenly he got up and galloped away.

But he wasn't going in the direction of home.

He was following the bus!

*   *   *

Traffic was heavy that morning, and the yellow schoolbus kept stopping and starting, producing groans and boos from all the kids. "Now don't be silly, children," said Miss Hollings. "It's still the rush hour, and the driver's doing the best he can. We'll get going quicker once we're out of town."

The bus drove on.

David's friend Tom was looking

thoughtful. "You know, David, I could have sworn I saw something just as we left."

"What sort of something?"

"Something big and white and hairy!"

David looked alarmed. "Not Goliath?"

"Well, it could have been some other big dog. I only caught a quick glimpse, just as we turned the corner."

David tried to look out of the back window, but he and Tom were sitting near the front, and the rows of heads kept getting in the way.

He stood up to get a better look, but Miss Hollings snapped, "Oh, do sit down, David! You're not usually such a nuisance—I can't think what's gotten into you this morning."

Hurriedly, David sat down.

Surely Goliath wouldn't have been

crazy enough to follow him to school?

David knew the answer to that question as soon as he asked it. Goliath was crazy enough for anything.

Still, thought David, if he had followed him, he'd surely have had the sense to go home when he saw he was too late.

Wouldn't he?

The bus drove on.

Soon, as Miss Hollings had

predicted, the traffic thinned, and they were able to pick up a bit of speed, driving along a country road lined with trees.

A big gas station appeared, and the driver pulled up outside it.

Miss Hollings sighed. "Now what?"

"We won't get far without any gas," said the driver.

There was a store attached to the gas station, and everyone started shouting at once. "Please miss, can we get out, miss? Can we buy some candy and some ice cream and some soda, miss? Please, miss, I need to use the bathroom!"

Miss Hollings sighed. "All right, all right, you can stop that noise. We'll have a ten minute break and you can all use the bathroom and go to the store!"

Everyone poured out of the bus.

There was only one bathroom, and by the time everyone who wanted to use it had used it, and by the time the lady at the counter had served everyone who wanted candy and drinks, and the driver had filled up the gas tank of the bus and paid for it, quite a long time had gone by.

Miss Hollings started herding everyone back on the bus. "Hurry along, you children, we're well behind schedule now . . ."

David was the last to get on the bus.

He was hanging back, staring down the road behind him.

"Not you again, David," said Miss Hollings impatiently. "Now what's the matter?"

"Look," said David simply. He pointed.

Miss Hollings looked. "I can't see anything . . . wait a moment, yes I can.

A sort of big white shape moving down the road toward us . . ." She turned to David. "You don't mean ..."

"I'm afraid so, Miss Hollings," said David. "It wasn't my idea, honestly!"

They stood and waited while the white shape grew larger and furrier and finally turned into Goliath, exhausted but determined, galloping down the road toward them.

With a final effort, he staggered up to David and collapsed exhausted at his feet, tongue lolling out.

All the kids on the bus gave a cheer!

They all climbed off the bus again, crowding around Goliath and making a huge fuss over him.

David persuaded the store lady to give him a bowl of water, and Goliath slurped it down happily.

Someone gave him some chocolate, and Goliath barked his thanks. He

wagged his tail and began running
around the group of excited children,
enjoying all the pats and strokes and
fuss he was getting, and hoping

someone else would give him more candy.

Goliath was having a wonderful time.

But Miss Hollings wasn't and neither was David.

"I'm really sorry, Miss Hollings," he said miserably. "It was all his idea— you know how silly he is!"

"Well, it's a touching example of doggy devotion, I'm sure," said Miss Hollings. She had a Yorkshire terrier called Scrap that she was devoted to herself. "The problem is, what do we do with Goliath? We could take him home, but that would lose us the rest of the morning. No, there's only one thing to do. Goliath will have to come with us to Foskett's Farm. We'll call your parents when we're there, David, and someone will have to come and take him home tomorrow.

The farm's not really all that far away!"

There was another cheer from the kids. "Good old Goliath. Goliath's coming to summer school!"

They all got back on the bus.

"Goliath likes to ride with his head out of the window," said David apologetically. "Otherwise he tends

to get carsick."

The bus set off, David sitting beside Goliath who had his head stuck out of the window, his fur streaming back in the breeze.

David sat quietly in his seat.

It was nice having Goliath with him, but he couldn't help feeling there was a lot more trouble in store.

Somehow Goliath always seemed to cause chaos wherever he went.

And David was right.

When they got to Foskett's Farm they heard all about the ghost. And that led to more fuss than David could ever have imagined . . .

Chapter Three

The Ghost of Foskett's Farm

"Ghost?" said Miss Hollings briskly. "What ghost?"

It was later that evening and they were all sitting around the fire in the big old-fashioned kitchen at Foskett's Farm. Mrs. Foskett was giving everyone big mugs of cocoa. It was just before bedtime. They'd had a busy and enjoyable day with a cross-country hike in the morning, a picnic in the fields, and a Pond Life study group in the afternoon.

This had been constantly interrupted by Goliath, who kept falling in the pond and having to be rescued.

Now he was stretched out steaming in front of the fire while the kids had their bedtime cocoa.

David's parents had been phoned and they had agreed to drive out to the farm the following evening and

take Goliath home.

"Please, tell us about the ghost, Mrs. Foskett," chorused the children.

Mrs. Foskett handed out the last mug of cocoa. "Oh, it's all a lot of nonsense really, my dears. Only Bill, our hired hand, swears that the back pasture is haunted. He says he saw a ghostly white shape one night, floating toward him. Now none of the farm hands will go near that pasture

nor by it after dark!"

Miss Hollings was fascinated and horrified at the same time. "What did

he claim to see?"

Mrs. Foskett lowered her voice. "He says he saw a great white shape, adrifting toward him and making strange howling noises . . ."

"Nonsense," said Miss Hollings briskly. "I expect he saw a sheep or a bush or something and frightened himself."

A voice said, "I saw what I saw. And it wasn't any sheep, nor any bush either. That was a ghost, that was. And if you know what's good for you, you'll stay safe indoors after dark."

They turned toward the voice and saw a scruffy-looking, unshaven man in the doorway.

"Now just you clear off, Bill, and stop frightening everyone," said Mrs. Foskett. "And just be sure you check that all those gates are shut before you turn in."

Bill turned and slouched away, and Mrs. Foskett and Miss Hollings were soon chatting about farm affairs.

Farmer Foskett, it seemed, was still in the farm office, trying to do his accounts. "No matter how hard he works, he doesn't seem to be able to make much profit," said Mrs. Foskett sadly. "We thought this was going to be a good year, but he tells me it looks worse than last."

Miss Hollings looked at her watch. "Off you go, boys and girls, we've a full day tomorrow. You know where your rooms are."

Everyone got up to go—everyone except Goliath, who had fallen asleep in front of the fire. They could hear him snoring. "You leave him there in the warmth, my dear," said Mrs. Foskett. "He can sleep in the kitchen. He'll be well enough there."

Mrs. Foskett had converted two attic rooms into dormitories, one for girls and one for boys. Miss Hollings was sleeping in one of the spare bedrooms that they used for bed-and-breakfast visitors.

"What about that ghost?" said Tom.

A boy called Ricky said, "Rubbish. I don't believe in ghosts." Ricky was a bit of a show-off.

"Oh, don't you?" said Tom. "Well, I bet you wouldn't dare go out to the back pasture and look for it!"

"Oh, yes, I would," Ricky instantly.

"Well, go then!"

"I will," said Ricky. "If you'll come with me!"

Tom was silent.

"What's the matter?" jeered Ricky. "Not scared are we?"

Tom started getting back into his clothes. " 'Course not. Anyone else

31

coming ghost hunting?"

No one moved. Tom looked appealingly at David. "What about you? You'll come won't you?

David thought the whole thing was silly. But he could see that Tom was a lot more frightened than he pretended to be, and you had to stand by your friends. "All right, I'll come. Just a quick look around and back again, though. I'm not hanging around all night."

No one else was interested. "I think you're all nuts," said another boy called Jeremy.

It was agreed that they'd wait till everyone was in bed, then creep downstairs, take a quick look at the back pasture—the big field just behind the farmhouse—and come straight back.

Just as midnight struck, David,

Ricky, and Tom crept downstairs, holding their rubber boots in their hands.

They could see Goliath fast asleep in the glow of the firelight. They crept

past without waking him. "Fine guard dog he'd make," thought David.

It was dark and spooky outside, with owls making sinister hooting sounds. Putting on their boots as quietly as they could manage, they made their way across the farmyard— it wasn't really dark once your eyes got used to it.

Ricky leaped back with a yell of

alarm as something white flapped out at him.

"It's only Mrs. Foskett's washing," said Tom. "There's a sheet on the line. I thought you said you didn't believe in ghosts!"

They crept cautiously across the yard. Like the fields beyond, it was dark and misty. Soon they were standing on the edge of the back pasture, a huge field that sloped away down toward the nearby river.

There were some sheep grazing on the other side. "There are your ghosts," said Ricky. "Miss Hollings was right—that old man saw a wandering sheep and frightened himself. Come on, you guys!"

Ricky marched confidently toward the middle of the field, disappearing from sight as the ground sloped downward into the mist.

"You coming?" asked Tom.

David shook his head. "Let him get on with it, the silly fool. He'll soon come back."

"Supposing he doesn't?"

"Then I'm going back to bed without him. I said I wasn't staying up all night. And I don't want to get caught, either. I'm in enough trouble with Miss Hollings as it is!"

They waited a few minutes, but there was still no sign of Ricky.

"We can't just leave him," said Tom.

"I suppose not," said David. "All right, let's go and bring him back."

They headed off into the mist, peering into it as they went, but there was still no sign of Ricky.

Suddenly David stopped. It's all right, I can hear him. He's running toward us."

"And he's yelling too," said Tom

rather uneasily.

As Ricky got nearer they could hear his voice. "Help, help! The ghost is after me!"

Seconds later Ricky appeared, dashing toward them.

"It's all right, we're here," said David. "What's the matter?"

Ricky's teeth were chattering so hard he couldn't talk. He turned and pointed. A huge white shape with glowing eyes was floating right toward them . . .

Chapter Four

Goliath Meets a Ghost

Goliath awakened with a start.

A distant shouting had interrupted his dream of chasing rabbits. Goliath looked around the kitchen.

David had disappeared again—after all the trouble he'd gone to find him!

And the kitchen door was open.

Yawning, Goliath ambled out to find his master . . .

*   *   *

David, Tom, and Ricky stood in a

huddled group in the middle of the dark and misty field.

For a moment they seemed frozen to the spot by sheer terror. Then Tom managed to croak, "Don't just stand here! Run!"

They turned and ran.

"Woo, woo, woo," wailed the ghost, and floated after them.

The three boys stumbled on. It was hard to get up speed because it was dark and the ground was all rough and rocky.

Ricky fell over twice, and the others

had to stop and heave him up.

David had a nasty feeling that the ghost was gaining on them. "Come on," he yelled, "we're nearly back at the farm—it won't follow us in there!"

("At least, I hope it won't!" he thought.)

The farmyard appeared out of the mist, with the dark shape of the farm buildings looming behind it.

Unfortunately, something else appeared too—another big white shape with a sort of long white cloak streaming out behind it. They skidded to a halt, all bumping into each other.

"It's another ghost!" yelled Ricky. "Now we're done for. We're trapped!"

Making a weird yowling noise, the second white shape shot past them and out into the field, rushing straight toward the first. Perhaps it was going to meet its friend, thought David. He

stared hard at the second shape as it
shot past.

"Wait a minute," he shouted. "That's
not a ghost. It's . . ."

The two ghosts crashed into one
another.

But it wasn't a silent, ghostly sort of
crash, it was a very real and solid one,
accompanied by a yell of pain and
fear, a strange baa-ing sound—and a
series of crashing barks!

Then there was pandemonium.

The sheep started to baa, cocks woke
up and crowed, the farm dogs in the

yard set off a chorus of howling, a horse in the stables whinnied, and distant cows began to moo.

Lights went on in the farmhouse, and after a moment yet a third white shape came hurtling toward them from the farmyard.

"Oh, no, not another ghost!" groaned Tom.

David stared hard and then grinned. "It's all right. That's not a ghost, either. It's Farmer Foskett in his nightshirt. He's got a shotgun. Let's go and see what's happening out in the field!"

Reassured by a bit of grownup backing, they ran back into the field.

The first white shape, now clearly just a man wrapped up in an old white sheet, was lying on the ground kicking and yelling, while the second was jumping all over it barking and growling loudly.

"Get him off!" the first shape was yelling in a muffled voice.

David ran forward and grabbed the

second shape by the collar and hauled it away. It was Goliath, of course, with something long and flowing draped around his neck. He barked excitedly, and licked David's face.

Farmer Foskett came pounding up, a strange sight in his nightshirt and rubber boots. He waved his shotgun.

"Now then, what's going on here!" he roared.

Suddenly, yet another white shape, a small and woolly one this time, had detached itself from the figure on the ground and was running across the field, baaing pathetically.

"That's one of my lambs!" growled Farmer Foskett.

He leaned over the shape on the ground, which looked up at him with a ghastly glowing face.

But Farmer Foskett wasn't scared. He reached down and pulled off the luminous ghost mask and the ragged sheet to reveal the shivering form of Bill, the hired hand . . .

*   *   *

"It was Bill all along," explained David next morning. "He dressed up as a ghost to stop people wandering around at night."

They were in the classroom where they had their morning lesson every day before leaving for nature study.

It wasn't a real classroom, just a room in the farm that had been sort of converted for them, with a table and chairs and a blackboard and books and pencils and things scattered around.

"Why would he want to do that?" asked Miss Hollings.

She'd slept through all the fuss last night, but the other children hadn't. There was no chance of getting on with the lesson till everyone had heard the full story.

"It's all a bit complicated," said David. "Luckily, Bill was so scared when we all caught him that he told Farmer Foskett everything."

"He's been stealing lambs, you see," announced Ricky. He'd recovered from his scare and was now his old show-off self again.

"Not just lambs," said David. "Chickens, eggs, bits of machinery, anything movable really. He'd been gambling, you see, and got into debt to another local farmer, a real bad group. Bill didn't have any money, so he was paying the debt off with anything he could steal from the farm. He nearly got caught several times, so he started the ghost story to scare everyone away."

"But didn't the Fosketts notice that

things were missing?" asked Miss Hollings.

"Not really—they're both a bit absent-minded. All they noticed was that their profits were down."

"And how did Goliath get involved?"

Goliath, who was stretched out by the door, thumped his tail at the mention of his name.

"He must have awakened and come out to look for me," explained David.

"Somehow he managed to get tangled up with Mrs. Foskett's wash line on the way, and he ended up with one of Farmer Foskett's nightshirts wound around his neck. I think he scared the

fake ghost even more than it scared all of us!"

"I wasn't scared," boasted Ricky, but no one took any notice.

David looked up at Miss Hollings. "So, it was a good thing Goliath was here after all, wasn't it?" he asked.

Miss Hollings smiled. "I quite agree, David. And so do Mr. and Mrs. Foskett. They're so pleased with Goliath that they want him to stay the whole week with us!"

A cheer went up from the class. "Good old Goliath!"

David bent down and gave Goliath a hug. "Serves you right, you silly old thing. Now you'll have to go to school for a week like me!"

Goliath wagged his tail and woofed gently.

He couldn't see why David made such a fuss about going to school. It seemed like quite a fun place to him. He stretched out by the door and waited for the lesson to end so they could go out and play in the sun.

Other *Adventures of Goliath* that you will enjoy reading:

About the author

After studying at Cambridge, Terrance Dicks became
an advertising copywriter, then a radio and television
scriptwriter and script editor. His career as a
children's author began with the *Dr Who* series and
he has now written a variety of other books on
subjects ranging from horror to detection.